The Hare and the Tortoise

based on a story by Aesop

Retold by Mairi Mackinnon

Illustrated by
Daniel Howarth

Reading Consultant: Alison Kelly
Roehampton University

Harry Hare loved running
more than anything in
the world.

3

Every morning, he woke
up and went for a run.

Then he ran to work,

ran around all day,

und ran home.

Everyone said he was the fastest hare around – maybe the fastest hare in history.

Harry, you're amazing.

6

Tom Tortoise worked
with Harry. All day long,
he heard Harry boasting.
He didn't think Harry was
so special.

I beat my
own record –
again!

Harry was always laughing at him. "Take your time, Tommy!"

One morning, Harry was feeling very pleased with himself. He ran to work in record time.

I really need some extra heavy shoes to slow me down!

"I must be the fastest creature in the world," he boasted. "Let's have a race to prove it."

Harry couldn't believe it when Tom Tortoise plodded over. "I'll race you, Harry," he said quietly.

"Tommy Slowcoach?
Are you serious?" asked
Harry. "You wouldn't even
get started!"

"I mean it," said Tom.
"Let's have the race next
Saturday at ten o'clock.
You choose where to race."

15

For the next few days, the animals talked about nothing else.

The story was in all the
newspapers.

It was even on television.

Harry trained extra hard.
He woke up early in the
mornings, and went running
in the evenings too.

He knew he would win,
but he wanted to win by
miles. He chose a good long
course for the race.

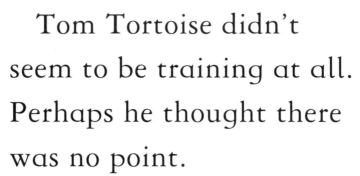

Tom Tortoise didn't
seem to be training at all.
Perhaps he thought there
was no point.

At last, Saturday arrived.
All Harry's friends came to
watch him race.

Tom's friends were there
too, but they didn't look
quite so happy.

23

It was a beautiful day.
Harry saw some television
cameras and did a little
running specially for them.

Tom just kept on talking
to his friends.

Soon it was time for the race to begin. Harry was already at the starting line. Tom slowly ambled over.

"On your marks, get set,
GO!" shouted the umpire.

27

Harry raced off and
disappeared almost at once.
Everyone laughed as poor
Tom plodded over the line.

As soon as he
was out of sight,
Harry stopped beside
a tree to rest.

Just...
need to... catch...
my breath...

29

After all his early
morning training, Harry
was very tired.

Nobody was looking. He had plenty of time to sit down for a while. He would still win the race easily.

31

His eyes started closing.
Why not have a nap? That
would make it even funnier
when he won the race.

He settled down in the
shade. Soon he was asleep.

Meanwhile, Tom Tortoise
was slowly making his
way along the course.

Most of the animals had
gone straight to the finish
line. Only Tom's friends
stayed with him.

Nobody saw Harry
sleeping under his tree.

35

Hours passed. The sun was setting and the air was cool.

Harry woke with a start.
Where was he?

37

Suddenly he remembered
the race. He hadn't meant
to sleep for so long...
but he could still
beat Tom.

Harry felt much better
after his nap. He did a few
stretches, then raced off.

He could see the finish line now. There was a huge crowd...

...and they were already cheering.

At that moment he saw a small, brown shell shape coming up to the line.

Harry felt cold all over. Surely that wasn't Tom?

41

He ran, faster than ever
before. Yes, he could do it!
The cheering grew louder
and louder.

Harry dived over the line,
but he was too late.

Tom Tortoise had won –
and he didn't even look out
of breath.

About this story

"The Hare and the Tortoise" is one of Aesop*'s Fables. These are a collection of short stories, first told in Ancient Greece around 4,000 years ago.

*say **Ee**-sop

Nobody knows exactly who
Aesop was, but the stories
are still popular today,
and they are known all
around the world.

The stories are
often about animals,
and they always have
a "moral" (a message
or lesson) at
the end.

The moral of the story
about the hare and the
tortoise is:

Slow and steady wins
the race.

Series editor: Lesley Sims

Designed by Samantha Meredith

First published in 2007 by Usborne Publishing Ltd.,
Usborne House, 83-85 Saffron Hill, London EC1N 8RT, England.
www.usborne.com
Copyright © 2007 Usborne Publishing Ltd.

48